Tiptoe Into Kindergarten

To the kindergarten teachers of the
M.E.D. Elementary School
—J.R.

Text and illustrations copyright © 1999 by Jacqueline Rogers.
All rights reserved. Published by Scholastic Inc.
SCHOLASTIC, CARTWHEEL BOOKS and associated logos are
trademarks and/or registered trademarks of Scholastic Inc.

No part of this publication may be reproduced, or stored in a retrieval
system, or transmitted in any form or by any means, electronic, mechanical,
photocopying, recording, or otherwise, without written permission of the
publisher. For information regarding permissions, write to Scholastic Inc.,
Attention: Permissions Department, 555 Broadway, New York, NY 10012.

Library of Congress Card Catalog Number: 98-45430
ISBN 0-590-46653-4

12 11 10 9 8 7 6 5 4   0/0 01 02 03 04

Printed in Mexico   49
First printing, August 1999

Tiptoe Into Kindergarten

by Jacqueline Rogers

SCHOLASTIC INC.

Cartwheel B·O·O·K·S ®

New York   Toronto   London   Auckland   Sydney
Mexico City   New Delhi   Hong Kong

Tiptoe, tiptoe,
no one's looking

I can be
so very still

Hiding, hiding,
I can watch now
what they're doing
all day long

First a big book—
what a BIG BOOK!
Yummy colors
I must touch

On the chalkboard
I make letters
Take my turn
when they are done

Now some block games
roll-big-dice games
I count numbers
1, 2, 3

Puzzles puzzles
I find places—
This will fit in here
somehow

Uh oh, uh oh,
got to go now—
Where's the bathroom?
over there

Washing hands
like Mommy tells me
Big kids do it, too,
I see

What's inside that
funny table?
Rice, they call it
I must try

Crawling crawling
I find cubbies
full of goody things
inside

Singing songs now
jumpy songs now
Clapping hands
and stomping feet

They eat snack
while I try smock on
Got to paint a
big fat sun

I feel sleepy—
Where is Mommy?
I'll curl up for
just a bit

What a nice place
sunny fun place
I'll be back
I hope real soon